A Giant First-Start Reader

This easy reader contains only 34 different words,
repeated often to help the young reader develop
word recognition and interest in reading.

Basic word list for *Double Trouble*

a	do	someone
act	double	talk
alike	in	the
and	is	this
are	it	Tim
ate	Jim	Tim's
beds	Jim's	trouble
broke	look	twins
call	made	was
cookies	mess	what
dish	now	you
	or	

Double Trouble

Written by Rose Greydanus

Illustrated by Roland Rodegast

Troll Associates

Library of Congress Cataloging in Publication Data

Greydanus, Rose.
    Double trouble.

    Summary: Twin brothers get mistaken for each
other, both in helpfulness and in trouble.
    [1. Twins—Fiction] I. Rodegast, Roland.
II. Title.
PZ7.G876Do   [E]   81-2358
ISBN 0-89375-529-X   AACR2
ISBN 0-89375-530-3 (pbk.)

This is Tim.

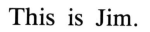

This is Jim.

Tim is Jim's double.

And Jim is Tim's double.

What do you call Tim and Jim?

Twins! Tim and Jim are twins.

Tim and Jim look alike.

Tim and Jim talk alike.

Tim and Jim act alike.

Someone made the cookies.

Was it Tim?

Or was it Jim?

Someone made the beds.

Was it Tim?

Or was it Jim?

Someone made the dish.

Was it Tim?

Or was it Jim?

Someone ate the cookies.

Was it Tim? Or was it Jim?

Someone made a mess.

Was it Tim? Or was it Jim?

Someone broke the dish.

Was it Tim? Or was it Jim?

Someone is in trouble.

Is it Tim? Or is it Jim?

What do you call Tim and Jim now?

Double trouble!